G000149149

Amber

A Fairy Tale

David Gibson

Text copyright © David Gibson 2014
Illustrations copyright © David Gibson 2014
All rights reserved.

David Gibson has asserted his right under the Copyright,
Designs and Patents Act 1988 to be identified as the author of
this work.

This book is a work of fiction. Names and characters are the
product of the author's imagination and any resemblance to
actual persons, living or dead, is entirely coincidental.
No part of this book may be reprinted or reproduced or
utilised in any form or by electronic, mechanical or any other
means, now known or hereafter invented, including
photocopying or recording, or in any information storage or
retrieval system, without the permission in writing from the
Publisher and Author.

First published 2014
By Rowanvale Books Ltd
2nd Floor
220 High Street
Swansea
SA1 1NW
www.rowanvalebooks.com

A CIP catalogue record for this book is available from the
British Library.
ISBN: 978-1-909902-87-9

Chapter 1

The Wandering Woods were vast and unimaginable in size. A canopy of ever changing shades of green stretched from the mountains of the cold north to the great river that wound its way far to the south. Trees, strong and proud, stood branch to bark with those that were old and gnarled, covering the land from the ocean in the distant west to disappear into the hazy depths of the fairy mists to the east.

Over this great expanse of forest a little finch flew with purpose, close to the very heart of the Wandering Woods, where the trees were all the brightest colours and shades, and where a little girl of no more than ten played happily within a garden of such natural wonder that, in turn, surrounded a cottage of equal beauty. The little girl was called Amber, and she was anything but an ordinary little girl.

The chirpy little finch with bright blinking eyes circled and landed on the open window ledge, right beside where Amber played. It watched her as it sang its lilting song and Amber hummed along with the tune while she bashed a battered old scarecrow, its straw innards sent into the wind with another sweep of her notched wooden sword.

A clatter of metal pans and the sound of breaking glass crashed through the open cottage window from within, followed by a cry of pain and a muffled curse. The finch flew off in haste and Amber stood up, gripping the ledge with grimy hands, her tip-toes in the mud beneath the sill.

"Mother?" she called, not quite able to see in through the high window frame.

"Amber!" she heard from somewhere inside. The girl, her blue eyes sparkling and her brown, twirled locks of hair streaming behind her, ran through the garden, sending butterflies and bees to flight and birds squawking up into the trees. She sped through the door like a fox into its hole and skidded to a halt, where her mother, Blossom, fair of hair and beautiful, lay on the floor in pain with tears upon her cheeks.

"It's all right Amber. Really, I fell. I suddenly became dizzy!" She brushed her tears and smiled up at her daughter. "Now help me up, my precious. I'll just have a sit down." And so Amber helped her to the chair with many cushions and a deep soft back that her mother liked best.

When her mother was settled, she said to her daughter, "Amber, I think I may need some of my potion. Be a dear and bring it for me, please." Amber did as she was asked, but when she found the dark green bottle, shaped like a bulb that hadn't yet sprouted, she found it to be empty. Her mother wasn't worried, though; she asked her daughter to fetch the last bottle, which she kept still in its box. Amber again obliged but, when she came back to tell her mother that the boxes were all empty, her mother's smile was not quite as reassuring as it had been.

"Will Aunty Belladonna not make you some more?" she asked.

Her mother then answered, the smile fading from her face altogether, "Belladonna is my sister, Amber, and I love her. When we were children she cast a curse on me, a careless thing, but deadly. In a tantrum and a rage she caused the need for my potion, and only in her domain can the ingredients be found." She tried to smile once more but didn't quite manage it. "She will not help me!"

The first thing that Amber felt at hearing those words was real sadness, but she was also angry. She knew that her mother had to take a special potion every day, yet until now she hadn't known the reason why. It did not take long for that anger to be replaced by determination; Amber was, after all, a very capable and clever girl. She said, "I will go. And I will find the ingredients you need, Mother!"

Blossom had closed her eyes, only momentarily to rest. Hearing her daughter's words, they sprang open again, alert and fearful. "You must not, Amber!" her mother told her. "She is both bitter and cruel. Alone and without the blessing of a daughter such as you. She cannot be trusted, you must not go!"

Amber did not promise, however, and neither did her mother ask her to. She brushed up the broken glass from the floor and replaced the pan, and when evening descended she helped her mother up the narrow, creaking staircase to her bed.

Dawn brought a sense of urgency to Amber. Her mother, too poorly to rise from her bed, ate a small amount of bread and cheese that her daughter provided, and then promptly fell into a troubled sleep. For as long as Amber could remember, the little green bottle had been a constant in her mother's daily routine. So much so that Amber had never asked about its contents. It was obvious to Amber that her mother couldn't make the two day journey herself. It was also apparent that Amber was the only person who could help her mother. If she didn't, she knew in her heart that her mother might die.

She put more bread and cheese on the plate beside her mother's bed, along with several juicy red apples. A large jug of water and a clay cup followed these, and lastly she placed a handwritten note on the pillow next to the sleeping woman, as an explanation for when she awoke. Then, the little girl packed a small, brown leather satchel of provisions for herself and, slinging it over her shoulder, left the house, picking up the battered wooden sword on the way and thrusting it snugly through her belt.

Chapter 2

It seemed to Amber, as she followed the winding path through the Wandering Woods, that the many colours and shades of the forest were not as vibrant and bright as they had been yesterday, and all the days before. The birds didn't sing so happily either, and the animals, normally so friendly and brave, didn't frolic and play or come to shake their tails at her. It was almost as if a held breath kept everything still and subdued.

"Or, do you share my concern?" she stopped and enquired of a rather shy hare, halfway out of his burrow, nose twitching and whiskers wobbling. "Do you love my mother also? As she surely loves you!" she said, turning to survey every tree and living thing. For a moment, a light wind rustled the leaves in the canopy above her and she imagined the sound a breathy, "Yes!"

She resumed her journey; there was no time to waste. The day was still new and fresh, but it would take most of it to reach her aunty's house. She had never been to Belladonna's home before, yet she knew this was the path that would take her there.

Morning turned to afternoon, and had progressed further still by the time the forest around Amber started to change. Brambles and weeds struggled with each other to reclaim the path and the abundant flora of the forest dwindled to an occasional splash of sickly colour, spotted with blight. She knew that she was now entering the domain of her aunt, Belladonna.

Crows and rooks were the only birds, calling savagely to each other from the trees above her head, and not once did she see any other animals of the forest. She scrambled and dodged her way, following the disappearing path through the gathering gloom, until evening approached and she stumbled from the forest into an area devoid of living trees. Each one was cut and splintered and rotting where they were felled; only the occasional twisted and stunted trunk survived. On the far side of this lifeless space, sitting close beside a murky pond, was a stone structure - grey, squat and unwelcoming. Only a trailing smudge of black smoke leaking from the lopsided chimney gave any impression of life within. "This must be Belladonna's home," Amber whispered to herself. She was a little scared after all.

It took a while to cross the treacherous clearing. Reaching the pond, its water brown and smelling like rotten eggs, she didn't venture close; with her nose all screwed up and wrinkled to block the horrible smell, she made straight for the front door of the bleak looking house.

Made of oak and banded with iron, it stood closed and impenetrable before her; a tarnished brass knocker, in the shape of some hideous animal's claw that she didn't recognise, hung level with her head, squeaking softly in the breeze. There were windows on this side of the house, though dark and soot stained and impossible to see through. Amber reached nervously and struck the knocker three times, and waited for her aunty to answer. She didn't have long to wait. The door flew open just seconds after she let go of the brass claw. A rush of warm, stale air gusted from within and billowing black robes swirled and coalesced into a figure in the open doorway.

"Who dares to darken my door?" the figure said, the voice dripping with venom. Raven black hair, darker than night itself, framed a face not unlike Amber's mother's, though much paler; instead of the kindness and honesty that radiated from the eyes of Blossom, Belladonna's were dark and reflected only malice. When they finally lowered to settle their gaze upon Amber, a touch of surprise crossed her shadowy features.

"A little girl!" she exclaimed, a pale hand shooting out from her robes, and grabbing hold of Amber's upper arm, long nails pinching through the fabric of her sleeve.

Surprised, rather frightened, and unable to struggle free, she said, "My name is Amber, Aunty Belladonna, and I am your sister Blossom's daughter." As soon as she said this, the grabbing, hurting hand was snatched back and disappeared once more within the robes as if bitten by a snake. Belladonna's intake of breath hissed between her teeth in shock, her dark eyes searching the face of the little girl who stood before her. Then, slowly and purposefully, her expression changed. The anger melted and her words softened in a sickly sweet way that did not fool Amber for one minute.

"Come in child, come in!" she said, with a forced and pretentious smile on her lips.

Amber smiled nervously as she was ushered into the gloomy house, the door behind her closing with a solid thump.

Her aunt's house, both inside and out, proved to be the complete opposite to the home she shared with her mother. Only the weakest light seeped through the stained and dirty glass windows, the main room brightened only by a spluttering fire in the stone hearth and a number of candles, wax pooling at their bases. Bushels of herbs and other ingredients hung from the ceiling, and scrolls and books lay on every surface. Animal skulls and assorted bones scattered the room, along with other items that were unfamiliar to Amber - some as if positioned for display, while others seemed haphazardly discarded.

"So, my sister has a daughter, does she?" the woman muttered.

Thinking that she was speaking to her, Amber replied, "Yes Aunty, and I'm sorry I have not visited before today, but my mother is very ill."

"Is she now?" Belladonna said, feigning concern.

"Yes she is, and she's in need of her potion but has run out. Will you make her some more, please Aunty, and I will take it to her?"

Belladonna did not answer straight away. She tapped her index finger gently upon her lips as she thought, and mumbled to herself under her breath, too quietly for Amber to hear. *"So, my sister has a child, and all these years has kept it from me. A pretty little thing, all innocent and wide eyed, and now she needs my help. The potion is a simple thing to make, the ingredients I have in abundance, yet what do I gain?"* She paced about the room now, lifting jars and shaking her head, a plan forming in her wicked mind.

"I shall make a potion, but it will not be for her mother - it will be for her, and when she tastes it she will forget everything." Reaching a decision, she said instead to her niece, who was waiting patiently for an answer, "Of course I shall help. But you will need to gather the ingredients for me as they are best when fresh!"

"Oh, thank you Aunty, I knew you would! Tell me where and what to fetch and I will gladly go," Amber replied, smiling with relief.

"Firstly, we will need Muddleroot from a goblin's garden, and secondly, Moonflower petals from the Shimmering Lake, and *finally* some fairy dust from the wings of a queen." As she told her niece what she required to brew the potion, Belladonna watched carefully to see if the little girl suspected anything, but Amber had no way of knowing that the items she agreed to fetch were not the ingredients of her mother's potion, but for something else entirely. When Amber asked where she was to look, her aunty pulled an old map from one of the many cluttered shelves lining the walls, and with ink and quill circled three areas on the brown crispy paper, then handed it to the little girl.

"Now quick, quick - there's no time to waste!" Belladonna told her, as she bustled her towards the door again and opened it. "Follow the path there!" she pointed, "and you will soon find the goblin village." And without further ado, Amber found herself outside and the door once more closed swiftly and firmly behind her. She wasn't entirely sure, but as she made to follow the path her aunty had shown her, she thought she could hear the cackle of cruel laughter coming from inside the house.

Chapter 3

The sun was high as Amber started along
the path, though only the occasional
bright beam shone through the forest's
oppressive canopy. Winding and turning,
the path meandered between the trees,
choked once more by overgrowing vines
and weeds. Amber sang softly to herself
as she walked, lightening her mood and
brightening the forest around her, or so it
appeared, until finally she could hear

other voices coming from somewhere ahead.

Not sure what to expect, she crept carefully, trying to avoid stepping on any twigs, or anything that might give her away. Before long the forest gave way to a little village. Tiny houses made of wood filled the clearing, some even built into the branches of the trees themselves.

This must be the goblin village, Amber thought, and true enough, the source of the voices she had heard on her approach were small men and women, slightly yellow in colour and none taller than she. Some were gardening in little plots while others simply chatted in passing, while children no taller than Amber's knee ran and played among their elders. She hid from sight behind a large bush at the edge of the forest that surrounded the little community, and tried to figure out what to do. Having never met a goblin, she wasn't sure if they were friendly or not, and indeed whether they would let her have some Muddleroot if she asked for it.

It was while she was hiding in this way that she heard a nervous cough from behind her and, turning about, came face to face with a goblin, who appeared to have been watching her for some time. Wearing short brown leggings and a green shirt, he took several steps backwards but did not run away.

"Hello," Amber said gently.

"Who are you? And what are you doing here?" the goblin asked, his words tumbling from his mouth almost too fast for Amber to understand.

"My name is Amber, and I'm looking for some Muddleroot. Can you help me?"

"Fiddlegrunt!" the goblin said.

"Pardon?"

"Fiddlegrunt; that's my name," he said, for the goblin looked and sounded like a boy, yet it was hard to tell. "What are you?" he asked.

"I'm a girl, a human girl, and it's very nice to meet you, Fiddlegrunt."

"Is it?" the little person said, cocking his head, and Amber replied that it was. They talked for a while, and during this time Fiddlegrunt lost his nervousness and came closer, eventually offering to help Amber with what she needed. "Stay here and I'll return to you quickly. My dad grows Muddleroot in his garden and I'm sure he won't miss a little." And with that, the goblin scampered around the bush and into the village, running as fast as he could - which was very fast indeed. A moment later he came back carrying a long brown root, newly pulled from the soil, and handed it to Amber proudly.

"Thank you, Fiddlegrunt, you're a good friend," she said, placing the root carefully into her leather satchel.

"Friend?" He looked confused.

"Yes, we're friends now, and friends help each other." The goblin pondered this new word that he hadn't heard before, and then nodded enthusiastically.

"Amber and Fiddlegrunt are friends!"

Evening was fast approaching, and with two items still to find, Amber told Fiddlegrunt that she really must be on her way, having already explained to him why she was on this quest for ingredients. Fiddlegrunt, however, had other plans; after all, he had never met a human that he liked before and now he had a friend.

"I'll come too, and help my friend!" he said.

"Oh Fiddlegrunt, you are a true friend!" Amber told him, and squeezed the goblin in a great big cuddle. The two of them then set off, with Fiddlegrunt leading the way. As they walked, they talked. Fiddlegrunt knew all about the good witch Blossom, whose voice soothed the forest and gave a helping hand to nature, and her evil sister whose spells and potions were used to hinder and transform things. Eventually he asked a very pertinent question.

"If your aunty is a bad witch and your mother a good one, then are you a witch also?" Amber had never really thought about it before, but started to now, and she found it a little worrying. If she was a witch, what kind would she be - good or bad?

The evening closed in about them while the two friends travelled together through the Wandering Woods. When it became too dark for Amber to see where she was going, the goblin held her hand and guided her, because everybody knows that goblins can see in the dark; with the moon now high in the sky, they quietly came upon the shore of the Shimmering Lake. Fiddlegrunt explained to Amber that the trees around the lake were the home of the Horrible Harpies, rude creatures that were half woman and half bird with foul mouths and nasty tempers. As they carefully crept closer to the edge of the lake, Fiddlegrunt pointed to several floating lilies, their petals newly open to greet the moon. They could also see several bulky shapes high amid the tree branches, where the Harpies made their nests. They squeezed themselves amid a prickly bush of thorns and un-flowered buds.

"If you are a witch just like your mother, then your magic will be in your voice," Fiddlegrunt explained to her. "If you sing a lullaby to them I'm sure it will work, and I can swim out into the lake and get the moonflower for you."

Amber thought this was a wonderful plan and she thanked the goblin again. "I will try. But what if I'm not a witch at all?" she asked her friend.

"But you must be, Amber, don't you see? I only hope there are no Water Sprites living in this lake, I don't like Water Sprites!"

So Amber started to sing, very quietly at first, an old lullaby that her mother used to sing when she was a baby. Suddenly, Fiddlegrunt sucked in a surprised breath and pointed at the little flower buds that surrounded Amber; they were starting to bloom in response to her song. He smiled reassuringly at her. "See, you are a good witch, just like your mother!" Amber felt such joy in her heart, and relief. Without another second, the goblin was gone from their hiding place and slowly inching into the water of the lake while Amber continued to sing, her voice now stronger and more confident. The Harpies snored and stretched but not one of them awoke as Fiddlegrunt reached the lilies and picked several flowers, holding them carefully in his mouth so that he could still swim.

Without warning there was a splash, and only bubbles on the surface where her friend had been. Amber stopped singing, worried for the little goblin, when all of a sudden his head popped up again, eyes wide and searching around while he tried to swim. Then, Amber saw the Water Sprite. A tiny figure, man-shaped but made entirely of water, dancing across the top of the lake. Again Fiddlegrunt disappeared below the surface as the sprite leapt and landed on the goblin's head, laughing and giggling in a shrill little voice.

Forgetting the slumbering Harpies for the moment, Amber sprang from her concealment and rushed to the edge of the lake. She grabbed several round pebbles from the ground and began throwing them at the sprite, but they passed right through his watery body with no effect. Fiddlegrunt was not far from the shore but was having terrible trouble trying to stay afloat, and there were noises coming from the trees now as the Harpies, released from Amber's magical voice, were waking. She splashed into the cold water, wading through the thick mud at its bottom until she was close enough to reach her friend. As he popped to the surface again, she grabbed his hand and yanked him from the water clean onto the bank, only just saving him from the claws of a swooping Harpy that cawed and cursed at them as they ran together into the forest.

Twigs and leaves and dirty, smelly feathers rained down on the pair as they raced through the forest hand in hand. The foul and twisted Harpies, diving and dodging between the trees, wings crashing and curses flying, pursued them for a long time until finally, exhausted and battered, they gave up and returned to their nesting ground.

Huffing and puffing, the two friends took a few moments to rest and catch their breath. "Are you all right, Fiddle-grunt?" Amber asked her friend, between gasps of air.

"I am now! Thank you for rescuing me from that nasty, horrible sprite."

"Well, that's what friends are for!" she answered, and he smiled warmly in return.

"At least we've been running in the right direction. We must reach the edge of the Fairy mist before dawn or we'll have no hope of finding the queen," the goblin said once he had his bearings. So, rested and once more breathing normally, they continued on their way.

Chapter 4

Several hours of walking brought with them a lightening sky as dawn fast approached, but both Fiddlegrunt and Amber's map assured her that they would make it just in time. They talked and laughed and shared what most friends do while they travelled, until, from some-where ahead of them, they heard a great booming noise and a crashing and breaking of timber as something large moaned and groaned, getting louder and louder the closer they came.

"Sounds like an ogre!" Fiddlegrunt told Amber, whose eyes opened wide with fear. "Don't worry. They're big and clumsy and not very clever but altogether quite nice when you get to know them," he explained.

It wasn't long before they could make out a huge man-like shape up ahead between the trees. At first it looked to Amber as if the ogre were trying to dance. It hopped and skipped and tried to catch one enormous naked foot with hands as big as shovels, and each time it would slip out of his grasp, sending the ogre crashing and groaning around a clearing of his own making. Broken branches and splintered trees surrounded the creature, and the foliage of the forest floor was flat and trampled. Now that they were closer they could also see that the ogre was not alone. Dozens of Fairies, no bigger than the smallest bird, flitted and flew on delicate wings around where the ogre stomped, their little voices buzzing yet indistinguishable amid the ruckus that the ogre made. Several broke away from the rest when they noticed Amber and Fiddlegrunt and flew towards them, chattering over the top of one another.

"You must stop him!" one said.

"You must help us!" another pleaded.

"He is ruining everything!" the last implored.

"It's Thundergut!" Fiddlegrunt told Amber, recognising the ogre now. "What is he doing?"

Two of the Fairies flew away to join the others, while the one that remained tried to explain. Though small and delicate, the Fairy was very beautiful, with green-tinted skin and hair, and wings that were nearly transparent. Upon her head sat a dainty little crown. "He's squashing the plants and breaking the trees and none of us can stop him! Will you help us, please?" the fairy begged them.

Amber looked to her friend who shrugged his shoulders, with no idea of what to do. "Well, we can try!" she told the Fairy, and they both stepped out into the clearing that the ogre had made, shouting at the top of their voices to try and get Thundergut's attention.

"It hurts, it hurts. Oh how it hurts!" the ogre boomed when he saw the goblin and the girl.

"What's the matter, Thundergut? You've gone and got the Fairy folk in a frenzy!" Fiddlegrunt said, when the ogre stopped crashing; Thundergut stood on one leg, trying to hop in place and shaking the ground each time he landed.

"I stepped on a thorn and I cannot get it out," he moaned, his lip quivering as a tear the size of a grape slid down the side of his bulbous nose.

"Oh Thundergut, I'll have that out in a flash!" said Amber. "Now, sit down and let me have a look."

Sniffing and sobbing, the ogre did as he was asked; with a loud boom his extremely large bottom hit the ground. She found the thorn without too much trouble and plucked it from an extremely large and swollen big toe. Holding it up for the ogre to see, she said, "Here it is, Thundergut, such a small thing to cause so much trouble."

The ogre wiped his tears and sniffed loudly with a rumble like thunder.

"Nasty, pointy thing!" he said, his eyes puffy and red. "Thank you little girl, you are very kind!"

"You're welcome, Thundergut," Amber replied.

Settling into the trees and the grass of the clearing, the Fairies watched as Amber took a clean white handkerchief from her pocket and bound it around the ogre's toe, tying it in place while the fairy with the little crown on her head alighted upon Amber's shoulder.

"I don't know what we would have done if you had not come along to help; we are also very grateful to you," the Fairy said, and Amber smiled in reply.

Then, noticing the crown for the first time she asked the Fairy, "Are you the Fairy Queen?"

"I am. Elenor is my name," the tiny voice said in her ear.

"I am so pleased to meet you, Queen Elenor, for it was you that we have travelled to see," Amber replied, then went on to explain her quest to find the ingredients for her mother's potion. When she had finished her telling, the queen flew from Amber's shoulder and hovered low above a green leaf that had fallen to the ground. She flapped her wings so fast that sparkles of shiny fairy dust fell from them and landed on the leaf, which she folded into a tiny packet to contain the dust and handed it to Amber.

"Here is what you wish for, though I fear the ingredients you have been sent to gather will not produce a healing potion. Belladonna is well known to me, and her mind is twisted and evil. Be wary of any advice she offers, Amber."

"Thank you, I will," she answered, taking the offered packet and placing it carefully in her satchel with the Muddleroot and Moonflower. Thundergut pushed himself back to his feet and tested the injured toe, beaming a huge smile when he realised that it caused no more pain.

Time was moving swiftly and, with all the ingredients now gathered, Amber knew she must be on her way.

"Thundergut help, Thundergut fast, Thundergut carry Amber and Fiddlegrunt!" the ogre boomed in a voice that shook more leaves from the trees, and sent a couple of Fairies tumbling from the branch where they sat. They soon flapped their wings and halted their fall, as the ogre gave them an embarrassed grin as an apology.

"Oh, that would be wonderful, thank you, Thundergut!" Amber replied.

After saying goodbye to the Fairy folk, the ogre picked her up and sat her on his shoulder, then lifted Fiddlegrunt and placed him snugly in his breast pocket. Then, with careful but massive strides, he loped through the forest much faster than the two friends could have done.

Chapter 5

By the time the sun had risen halfway into the sky above the forest, a familiar bad smell assaulted their noses, and Amber knew they were drawing close to Belladonna's house once more. Thundergut slowed his pace - fear of the witch outweighing his wish to help the little girl. He stopped short of the tree line that surrounded the dark and dismal cottage and helped the two friends down, placing them safely on the ground at his feet.

"Thundergut scared," he tried to whisper; the sound like a hundred bees humming his words. Fiddlegrunt also looked nervous and afraid, but he tried to hide it with a smile.

"It's ok, there's no need to come any nearer; you've both done so much for me already."

To which they both looked relieved, but Fiddlegrunt, being an unusually brave little goblin, said, "We will wait for you here at the edge of the trees, and when you leave we shall leave together." The ogre's eyes grew a little wide at the thought of being so close to the bad witch, yet nodded his agreement. Each received a huge cuddle in return before Amber strode out of the trees holding her nose, circled the foul pond and made her way to the door of her aunt's house.

Before she had even reached for the ornate knocker, the door swung wide and Belladonna was before her. "Do you have them?" she asked, her pale bony hand outstretched expectantly.

"I do, Aunty," Amber told her, offering the leather satchel and its precious contents, which was snatched from her grasp and carried inside, leaving Amber to follow.

"Sit by the fire and warm your bones, girl, while I brew you some tea." Belladonna told her, "I have some sad news."

"My mother?" Amber asked, tears springing to her eyes.

"Yes, I'm sorry but she died in the night, you took too long to find what I needed."

"No, she cannot be! Please, she can't have died!" she sobbed, but her aunt only nodded while she began to unpack the contents of Amber's satchel, sniffing each in turn.

Over her shoulder she spoke once more to her niece, "Never fear girl, you're not alone, you shall live here with me in my home." However, there was no sympathy in her words or care for her broken heart, and Amber found herself running from the house, stumbling, with tears falling to the ground as she went.

"I shall call when your tea is ready, girl; be quick to return when you have done with this crying!" But, running as she was, Amber didn't see the cruel smile that Belladonna showed. She tripped and fell and lay there sobbing, just a little way short of the edge of the forest.

"Amber?" a small voice said, but she did not hear. "Amber!" it repeated, and this time she raised her head, her eyes red and puffy, and looked into the trees. There she saw her friends, Fiddlegrunt and Thundergut who, though afraid of the witch, had come closer when they heard her crying. "What is the matter, Amber?" the little goblin asked, and through her tears she told them about her mother, and then let her head fall to the moss-covered ground once more with a new bout of sobbing.

Fiddlegrunt looked confused and Thundergut looked at his feet. "But that cannot be!" her friend said with certainty, and at his words Amber once more raised her head. "If the good witch Blossom were dead, then even the trees would know. The flowers and bees, the birds, and even me! The Wandering Woods would tell us so in the falling of the leaves and in the wind that shakes the trees," the goblin told her, without a shadow of doubt.

As her friend spoke, she felt his words were true, and knew that he must be right. She wiped her tears away with her sleeve and, after a few breaths to steady her voice, she spoke again. "But why would my aunt lie to me, Fiddlegrunt? How could she be so cruel?"

"Because she is bad, Amber, from her head to her toes, and I suspect that she has something up her sleeve too," the goblin answered her.

"My mother is alive," Amber said, and just like before, a soft breeze answered her with a breathy,

"Yes!"

From the house, Belladonna called, "Girl, your tea is brewed, come into the cottage and share a cup with me."

Fiddlegrunt and Thundergut melted once more into the trees, hiding from sight with a final word of warning to their friend, "Be careful!"

Feeling reassured and her grief forgotten, Amber got up, brushed the dirt and moss from her clothes and made her way back to the house. Concealing both her hope and anger from Belladonna, she walked through the open door and took a seat by the fire on a rickety old wooden rocking chair. She was suspicious of her aunt and knew now that she could not be trusted, but her mother was still in desperate need of the potion that only Belladonna could make, and so she sat and waited, all the while trying to figure out what her aunt had planned. With a fake smile, her aunt brought two cups to the fire, placing one on the little table next to Amber, and, taking a seat herself, placed her own identical cup on the same table beside where she sat.

"Now drink your tea and we'll have no more tears," Belladonna said, taking a sip from her own steaming cup and replacing it on the table, her scheming eyes never leaving her niece's face. But Amber was not fooled. She had seen what was left of the ingredients that she had gathered, discarded on a chopping board next to the kettle. She remembered what the Fairy Queen had told her about those items. Though she had no idea what purpose they were truly for, she suspected that they had been used to make the brew that now sat untouched beside her.

"Could I trouble you for some honey in my tea please, Aunty?" asked Amber, and when her aunt got up from her chair to fetch it, barely hiding the scowl that crossed her face, Amber quickly switched the cups around without the other woman noticing.

"Not too much now, it's hard to come by," Belladonna said, returning to her seat with a small clay jar that contained the sticky sweet honey. Amber spooned a dollop into her cup and stirred, all under the watchful eyes of her aunt, then, without showing her nervousness, she took a sip.

"Good," Belladonna said, "very good!" and took a long sip herself from the cup that had been intended for Amber.

So far, so good, Amber thought, but she still had no idea how to get the potion for her mother. She started to hum quietly while she thought, not realising what she was doing.

"Stop that!" her aunt told her before taking another sip from her cup, but Amber did not stop, because she had an idea.

"Stop it, I said!" Belladonna repeated, but Amber only hummed a little louder. Small shoots of green began to appear from out of the floor at Belladonna's feet and under her chair, but the witch didn't notice; they grew and twirled and crept around her ankles as Amber hummed, getting thicker and stronger by the second.

"Stop it at once!" she shot angrily, and started to rise to her feet, but Amber still did not stop. The tendrils and vines growing out of the floor suddenly burst upwards and around Belladonna, looping around her thighs and arms and even around her waist as Amber used the magic of her voice. They pulled Belladonna back into her chair and wound around and around, until the witch was incapable of moving a muscle – all but her head.

Only then did Amber stop her song.

"What have you done, you horrible child? Release me immediately!' her aunt demanded.

But instead, Amber made her own demand, "Tell me how to make my mother's potion, and only then will I set you free!"

"Your mother is gone!" Belladonna spat, "and you will soon forget," she went on, her face contorted with rage. "That brew that you've been drinking will take all your memories away, and you will not even remember your mother's name!" she cackled.

Amber smiled, "The tea that I've been drinking is not the tea that you gave me.

I switched the cups when your back was turned; so it is you who will forget!"

"No!" the wicked witch cried, struggling to break free of the vines and ivy that held her to her place.

"Now, tell me how to help my mother and I will set you free," Amber said.

Belladonna struggled and strained, but finally she agreed. "On the very top shelf, behind the lizard skull, you will find a bottle of your mother's potion; now set me free!" she finally said.

Amber reached up to the shelf by standing on a chair, and, moving the peculiar skull aside, she found a dark green bottle shaped like a bulb that hadn't yet sprouted, which contained her mother's potion.

"Now...now..." Belladonna began to say, "Now what am I doing here, and why do I look like I've taken root!" she finally said, her anger replaced with confusion.

Amber got down from the chair and came to stand before her aunt, the bottle clutched safely in her hand. The brew had finally worked its spell and Belladonna could remember nothing. "Hello, Aunt Belladonna,' Amber said.

"Hello," the woman replied. "Belladonna, is that my name?"

"Yes it is, and I'm Amber, your niece." She smiled at her aunt, and the smile she got in return warmed her heart. Amber started to hum again and as she did, the vines and shoots and ivy slowly withdrew, leaving the woman free to move once more.

When she could stand again, she looked around at what had once been her home and asked, "Tell me Amber, where are we?" When Amber explained that this was her house, her aunt just shook her head and said, "What an ugly dark place, my home? Well, I shall have to do something to brighten it up, I think!"

Amber gave her aunt a great big hug and told her that she had to leave, because her mother needed her, but she would return to visit soon. Then, she gathered her leather satchel, placed the bottle snugly inside and, waving good-bye, left the house to look for Fiddlegrunt and Thundergut.

She found them just beyond the tree line, worried and afraid but eager to know what had happened in the house. "Come on, I'll tell you on the way," she told them, and as they walked she began to explain everything that had happened within the dark and dismal cottage, but not before they all heard the sound of singing coming happily from inside.

Chapter 6

With the need for haste, once again Thundergut plucked Amber from the ground and settled her carefully on his shoulder, and fitted Fiddlegrunt snugly into his breast pocket. They were able to travel faster this way - the ogre's long strides swallowing the distance faster than their shorter legs could hope to. Even so, by the time the cottage that Amber shared with her mother, Blossom, came into view, it was growing late and the sun was beginning to dip beyond the forest's leafy shroud. The flowers that surrounded the cottage, once so beautiful and full of colour, were wilted now, their petals dry and scattered about the garden and crunching under foot on the path that led up to the front door. All was still and quiet as Amber climbed down from Thundergut's shoulder and approached alone, through the door and up the stairs to her mother's room.

There she found her, eyes closed as if asleep, just as she had left her, though her skin was white as snow. With eyes brimming with tears, and fearing that she had not returned in time, Amber climbed onto the bed beside her mother and removed the little green bottle from her satchel. From it she poured three drops between her mother's lips, then snuggled in against her and, before long, fell asleep herself.

When morning came, all bright and new, a little finch came with it, flying through the garden and alighting on the ledge of the open bedroom window, where a little girl and her mother lay sleeping side by side. It began to sing a song so happy and chirpy, welcoming the day with a heart full of joy, and the little girl's eyes slowly fluttered open, awoken by the bird's pretty singing.

Amber blinked, and for the briefest of moments the troubles of the last couple of days were forgotten, but soon her dreams left her and she remembered where she was. Then, she turned away from the open window and the little bird singing gaily to look at the woman beside her, and there was her mother looking right back at her, a smile on her lips and as beautiful and radiant as ever.

"Mother!" she gasped, "it worked!"

"I feel fine Amber, my clever little girl, but where did you find this bottle of potion?" Blossom asked, picking up the little green bottle that had rested between them all night.

Amber smiled the biggest smile and said, "It's a very long story, Mother, but first come downstairs. I have two very good friends that I would like you to meet."

Blossom, who was at first a little wobbly on her legs, having been in bed for several days, was helped down the narrow staircase by her daughter, and as they reached the bottom Fiddlegrunt was there to meet them, hopping and skipping on the spot, happy to see Amber's mother recovered and well.

"And who is this?" Blossom asked her daughter, smiling at the little goblin as she did.

"This is Fiddlegrunt, Mother; he's a very good friend. Fiddlegrunt, this is my mother, Blossom."

"I'm very pleased to meet you!" he said, finally standing still. Just then, a huge head with a bulbous nose, shaggy hair and a smile as wide as a letterbox popped through the open front door, quite surprising Amber's mother.

"And this is Thundergut," she said with a giggle, "another very good friend of mine, Mother."

"Well, it's very nice to meet you both," the good witch told the goblin and the ogre.

The three good friends and Blossom sat for a long time within her garden while they told her the tale of their adventures together, and as they did the little finch continued to sing chirpily from the windowsill. Many other animals once more returned to the vicinity of the cottage; rabbits scampering and butter-flies fluttering, and all the while, as if by magic, which of course it was, new flowers bloomed everywhere around them, filling the garden with colour and beauty again.

Blossom was amazed at all the things her daughter had accomplished with the help of her new friends, and she was also very proud. "And my sister remembers nothing of who she was?" the good witch Blossom asked her daughter when the tale was told in full.

"No, Mother, she is not a bad witch at all now!"

And as if to prove her point, who do you think came strolling from the edge of the forest, still looking slightly confused? It was Belladonna; no longer wearing robes of black, but a pretty green dress and a flower in her hair, and when she saw her sister and her niece she smiled, waved, and came right over.

Blossom stood, shocked and open mouthed, at the transformation of her sister as she glided through the garden towards them, her surprise so acute that she was unable to speak.

Smiling still, Belladonna nodded a greeting, first to the goblin and then to the ogre, and then hugged Blossom and Amber in turn. "I'm so glad to see that you are all right Blossom, Amber told me you were poorly so I left right away! Though I seem to have gotten lost several times," she laughed.

"See?" Amber whispered to her mother, and indeed Blossom could see that what her daughter said was true. Belladonna had forgotten everything that had made her bad.

Author Profile

David Gibson currently lives in North Wales after relocating in 2002 from Grasmere in the beautiful Lake District. He then began 'The Wandering Woods Series' whilst studying for an English and Creative writing degree at Glyndwr University, Wrexham, after spending many years attempting to write a series of fantasy novels. Having two children (a daughter aged six, and a son aged three), David drew his inspiration for *Amber: A Fairy Tale* from the two of them, and originally wrote 'The Wandering Woods Series' as bedtime stories for his children. Much of his daughter is within the character of Amber, and his son prevails within the planned third book of the series. *Amber: A Fairy Tale* is the first of a series based in the fictional realm of the Wandering Woods. David is also working on several adult novels and screen plays, as well as the next instalments in 'The Wandering Woods Series'.

Publisher Information

Rowanvale Books provides publishing services to independent authors, writers and poets all over the globe. We deliver a personal, honest and efficient service that allows authors to see their work published, while remaining in control of the process and retaining their creativity. By making publishing services available to authors in a cost-effective and ethical way, we at Rowanvale Books hope to ensure that the local, national and international community benefits from a steady stream of good quality literature.

For more information about us, our authors or our publications, please get in touch.

www.rowanvalebooks.com
info@rowanvalebooks.com